MY 1ST GRAPHIC NOVEL®

First Day, NO WAY!

MY FIRST GRAPHIC NOVELS ARE PUBLISHED BY STONE ARCH BOOKS
A CAPSTONE IMPRINT
151 GOOD COUNSEL DRIVE, P.O. BOX 669
MANKATO, MINNESOTA 56002
WWW.CAPSTONEPUB.COM

Library of Congress Cataloging-in-Publication data is available on the
Library of Congress website.

ISBN: 978-1-4342-2015-8 (library binding)

Summary: Kaylee and Jenna have always been in the same class — until this year.
Without Jenna by her side, Kaylee has a bad case of the first-day blues.
Will anything, or anyone, cheer her up?

Art Director: BOB LENTZ
Graphic Designer: EMILY HARRIS
Production Specialist: MICHELLE BIEDSCHEID

First Day, NO WAY!

by Lori Mortensen

illustrated by Rémy Simard

STONE ARCH BOOKS
a capstone imprint

How To Read
A GRAPHIC NOVEL

Graphic novels are easy to read. Boxes called panels show you how to follow the story. Look at the panels from left to right and top to bottom.

Read the word boxes and word balloons from left to right as well. Don't forget the sound and action words in the pictures.

The pictures and the words work together to tell the whole story.

Kaylee and Jenna are best friends.

They jump rope together.

They ride bikes together.

They tell jokes together.

A week before school started, class lists were sent out. Kaylee grabbed her mail. Jenna grabbed her mail.

They raced to their meeting spot at the park.

Kaylee looked for Jenna's name. Jenna looked for Kaylee's name.

Kaylee and Jenna were in different classes.

School wasn't going to be any fun at all.

On the first day of school, Kaylee went to one room. Jenna went to a different room.

Kaylee sat at a new desk. She got new books.
She got new pencils.

But nothing was fun without Jenna.

This year, Kaylee sat by Maggie. Kaylee knew Maggie, but not very well.

Maggie wore red glasses.

She wore necklaces made of gum wrappers.

She wore mismatched socks!

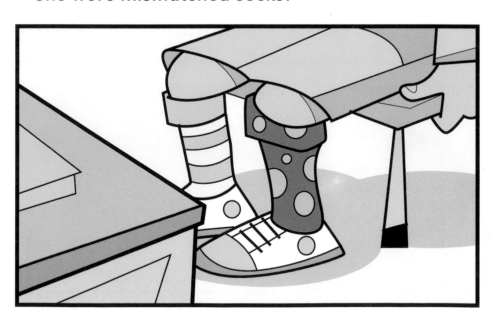

Maggie talked to everyone, and she talked a lot.

Kaylee slumped down in her chair. She liked
Maggie, but Maggie wasn't Jenna.

Kaylee watched the clock. Soon it would be recess. Then she'd get to play with Jenna.

They would talk. They would laugh. They would tell jokes.

Before the bell rang, it began to rain.

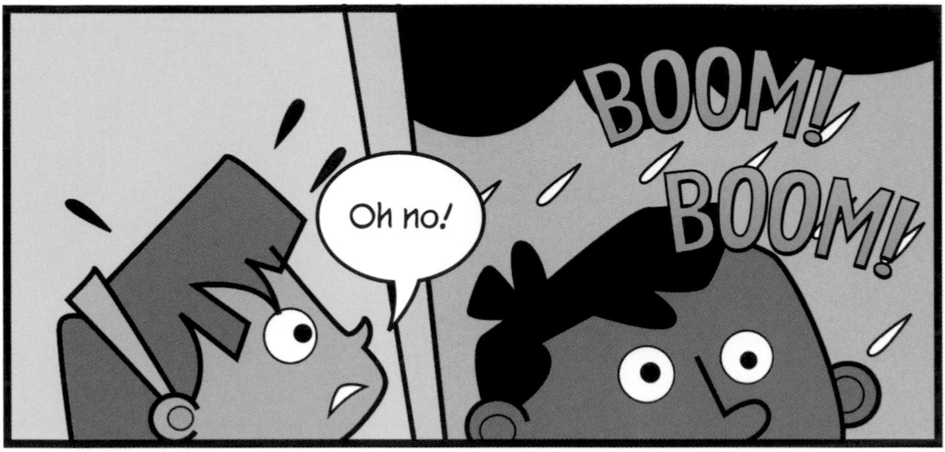
Oh no!
BOOM!
BOOM!

The other kids were happy to stay inside, but Kaylee was disappointed.

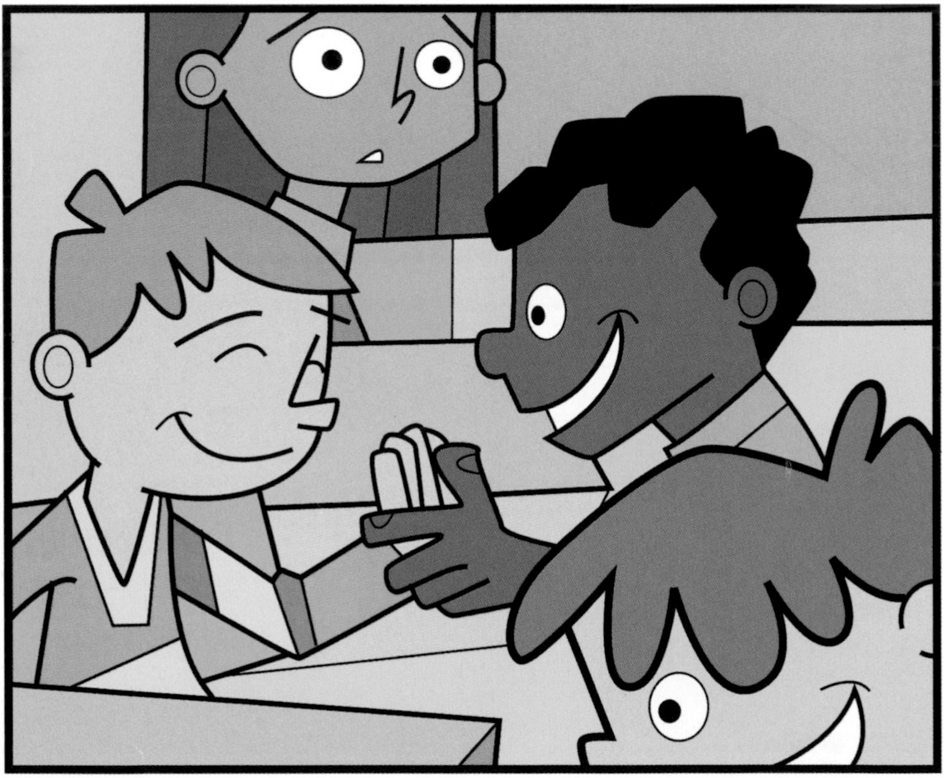

Recess was ruined! Her whole day was ruined!

Kaylee started to cry. Maggie pulled out the chair next to her and sat down.

SQUEAK

Then Maggie told Kaylee a joke.

Kaylee smiled. She didn't know Maggie liked jokes. In fact, she didn't know much about Maggie at all.

Kaylee, Jenna, and Maggie sat together at lunch.

They had fun talking, laughing, and telling jokes.

They made necklaces out of gum wrappers. It was going to be a good year after all.

The End

Lori Mortensen is a multi-published children's author who writes fiction and nonfiction on all sorts of subjects. When she's not plunking away at the keyboard, she enjoys making cheesy bread rolls, gardening, and hanging out with her family at their home in northern California.

Rémy Simard began his career as an illustrator in 1980. Today he creates computer-generated illustrations for a large variety of clients. He has also written and illustrated more than 30 children's books in both French and English, including *Monsieur Noir et Blanc*, a finalist for Canada's Governor's Prize. To relax, Rémy likes to race around on his motorcycle. Rémy resides in Montreal with his two sons and a cat named Billy.

GLOSSARY

DISAPPOINTED (diss-uh-POINT-ed) — feeling let down

MISMATCHED (MISS-macht) — things that don't go together

RECESS (REE-sess) — a break from schoolwork

RUINED (ROO-ind) — spoiled or wrecked

SLUMPED (SLUHMPT) — sat with shoulders bent forward

DISCUSSION QUESTIONS

1. Kaylee and Jenna think it's not fair that they are in different classes. Discuss a time when you felt like things weren't fair.

2. Kaylee and Jenna like to tell jokes. Make up your own joke and share it with your friends.

3. Is it hard to make new friends? Why or why not?

WRITING PROMPTS

1. Make a list of at least five activities you do with your best friend.

2. The first day of school can be scary. Write a paragraph describing how you felt on your first day of school.

3. Write a paragraph about how you met your best friend.

The First Step into GRAPHIC NOVELS

These books are the perfect introduction to the world of safe, appealing graphic novels. Each story uses familiar topics, repeating patterns, and core vocabulary words appropriate for a beginning reader. Combine the entertaining story with comic book panels, exciting action elements, and bright colors and a safe graphic novel is born.

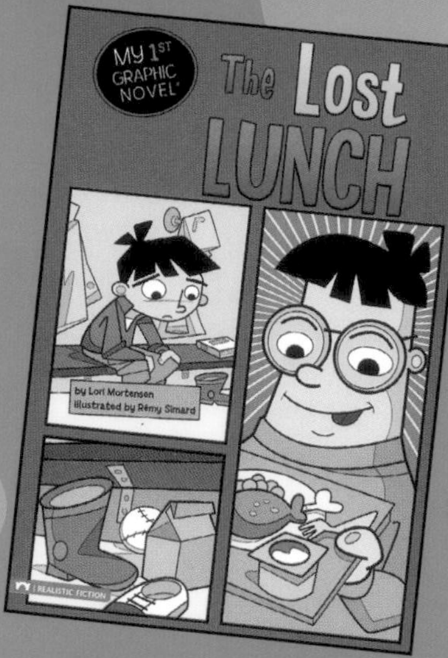
MY 1ST GRAPHIC NOVEL
The Lost LUNCH
by Lori Mortensen
illustrated by Rémy Simard
REALISTIC FICTION

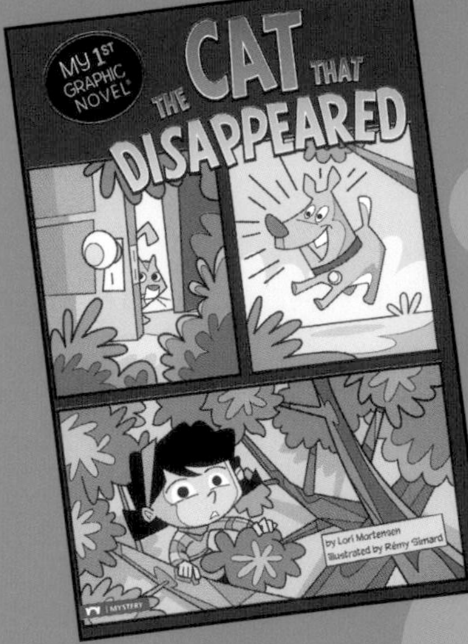
MY 1ST GRAPHIC NOVEL
THE CAT THAT DISAPPEARED
by Lori Mortensen
illustrated by Rémy Simard
MYSTERY

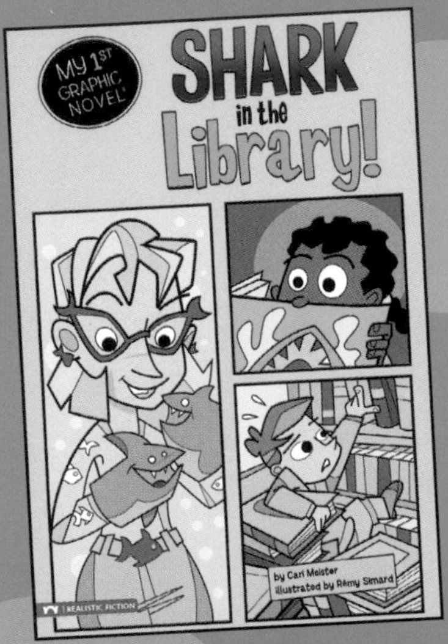
MY 1ST GRAPHIC NOVEL
SHARK in the Library!
by Cari Meister
illustrated by Rémy Simard
REALISTIC FICTION

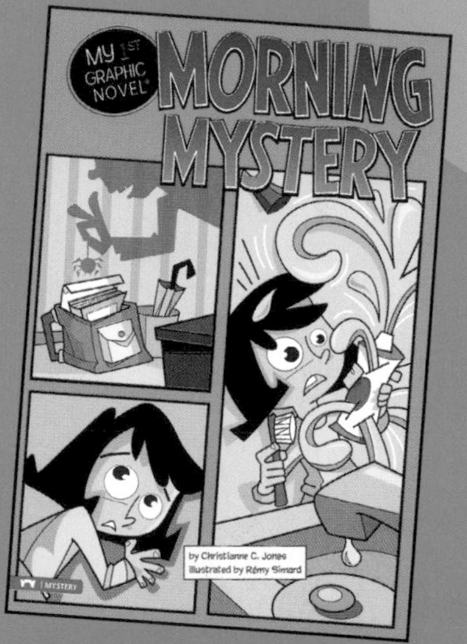
MY 1ST GRAPHIC NOVEL
MORNING MYSTERY
by Christianne C. Jones
illustrated by Rémy Simard
MYSTERY

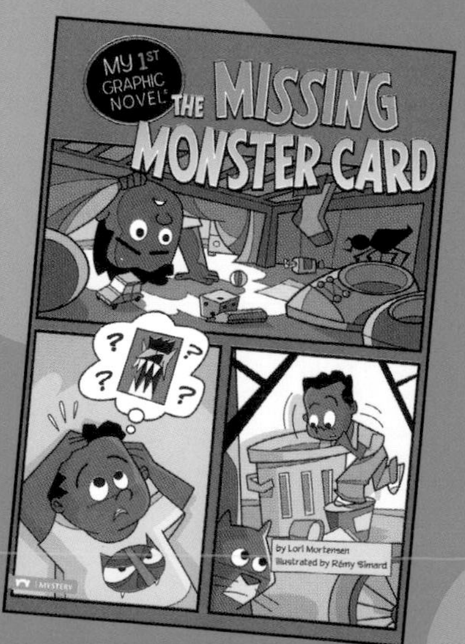
MY 1ST GRAPHIC NOVEL
THE MISSING MONSTER CARD
by Lori Mortensen
illustrated by Rémy Simard
MYSTERY

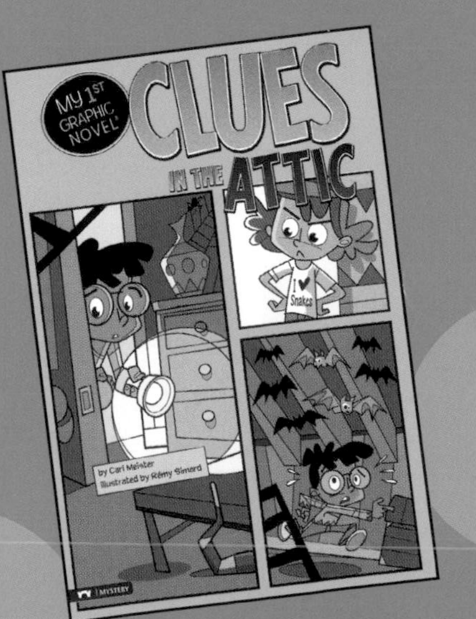
MY 1ST GRAPHIC NOVEL
CLUES IN THE ATTIC
I ♥ Snakes
by Cari Meister
illustrated by Rémy Simard
MYSTERY